Franklin's Reading Club

From an episode of the animated TV series *Franklin*, produced by Nelvana Limited, Neurones France s.a.r.l. and Neurones Luxembourg S.A., based on the Franklin books by Paulette Bourgeois and Brenda Clark.

Story written by Sharon Jennings.

Illustrated by Sean Jeffrey, Mark Koren and Alice Sinkner.

Based on the TV episode *Franklin's Reading Club*, written by Brian Lasenby.

 ™ Kids Can Read is a trademark of Kids Can Press Ltd.

Franklin is a trademark of Kids Can Press Ltd.
The character Franklin was created by Paulette Bourgeois and Brenda Clark.

ISBN 0-439-41817-8

12 11 10 9 8 7 6 5 4 3 2 1   3 4 5 6 7 8/0

Printed in the U.S.A.   23

First Scholastic printing, September 2003

Edited by Tara Walker and David MacDonald.

Franklin's Reading Club

SCHOLASTIC INC.

New York   Toronto   London   Auckland   Sydney
Mexico City   New Delhi   Hong Kong   Buenos Aires

Franklin can tie his shoes.

Franklin can count by twos.

And Franklin can read all by himself.

Most of all, Franklin likes to read

the Dynaroo books.

He has every Dynaroo book ever written.

One day, Beaver said, "Guess what?

There's a new Dynaroo book!"

"What's it called?" asked Franklin.

"*Dynaroo and the Monster,*" said Beaver.

"Ooooooh!" said everyone.

"It will be in the stores tomorrow,"

said Beaver.

Everyone agreed to meet

at Mr. Heron's bookstore.

"Let's go first thing in the morning,"

said Franklin.

"And let's wear our Dynaroo capes!"

But first thing in the morning

was too late.

"I'm all sold out

of *Dynaroo and the Monster,*"

said Mr. Heron.

"But we really wanted

that book," said Franklin.

"So did everyone else,"

said Mr. Heron.

Just then, Franklin saw Mr. Mole.

He had a copy

of *Dynaroo and the Monster.*

"Where did you get that book?"

asked Franklin.

"At the toy shop," said Mr. Mole.

"It's for my grandson."

"TO THE TOY SHOP!" shouted Franklin.

Franklin and his friends

ran down the street.

They ran around the corner.

They ran up the next street.

They ran and ran

until they got to the toy shop.

There was a sign in the window. It said

ALL SOLD OUT OF *DYNAROO AND THE MONSTER.*

Everyone groaned.

Just then, Franklin saw Mrs. Muskrat.

She had a copy

of *Dynaroo and the Monster*.

"Where did you get that book?"

asked Franklin.

"At the library," said Mrs. Muskrat.

"It's for my grandson."

"TO THE LIBRARY!" shouted Franklin.

Franklin and his friends

ran up the street.

They ran around the corner.

They ran down the next street.

They ran and ran

until they got to the library.

"Sorry," said Mrs. Goose.

"Mrs. Muskrat borrowed my last copy

of *Dynaroo and the Monster*."

Everyone groaned.

Franklin pulled off his Dynaroo cape.

"I'm going home," he said.

"Me too," said everyone else.

When Franklin got home,

his granny was there.

"Look what I bought my grandson!"

she said.

She held up *Dynaroo and the Monster*.

"Wow!" said Franklin.

"Thank you, Granny!"

Franklin put on his Dynaroo cape.

He opened his book

and read page one.

The phone rang.

It was Bear.

"Do you want to play?" asked Bear.

"No," said Franklin. "My granny gave me

Dynaroo and the Monster."

"Wow!" said Bear.

"Can I read it

after you?"

"Yes," said Franklin.

He sat down and read page two.

There was a knock at the door.

All of Franklin's friends were outside.

"Are you finished

Dynaroo and the Monster yet?"

asked Fox.

"Can I have it now?" asked Bear.

"What's taking you so long?"

asked Beaver.

"How can I read

if you won't leave me alone?"

Franklin said.

He closed the door and sat down.

Franklin read page three.

He looked up.

His friends were watching him

through the window.

Franklin looked down.

He read page four.

"I can't stand it!" shouted Beaver.

"You are a slow reader!"

Franklin pulled the curtains.

Franklin read page five

and laughed.

He got up

and went outside.

"Guess what happens

on page five," he said.

"DON'T TELL!" everyone shouted.

"You'll ruin the story!" said Beaver.

Franklin went back inside.

He could hear his friends

playing outside.

He opened the door.

"Are you finished?" asked Beaver.

"No," said Franklin. "I am not finished.

I will never finish

with all of you bothering me.

So please come in and sit down."

Everyone went in and sat down.

"What's going on?" asked Beaver.

"Welcome to Franklin's Reading Club,"

said Franklin.

"I will read *Dynaroo and*

the Monster out loud."

"Hooray!" said everyone.

"Chapter One," began Franklin.

"The Monster Says Boo!"

"Ooooooh," said everyone.

And then, no one made another sound

until Franklin said ...

"The End."